EDGE BOOKS™

Revised and Updated
War Planes
High-Altitude Spy Planes
The U-2s

by **Bill Sweetman**

Consultant:
Raymond L. Puffer, PhD, Historian
Air Force Flight Test Center
Edwards Air Force Base, California

Capstone

Edge Books are published by Capstone Press,
151 Good Counsel Drive, P.O. Box 669, Mankato, Minnesota 56002.
www.capstonepress.com

Library of Congress Cataloging-in-Publication Data
Sweetman, Bill.
    High-altitude spy planes: the U-2s / by Bill Sweetman — Rev. and updated.
    p. cm. — (Edge books. War planes)
    Includes bibliographical references and index.
    ISBN-13: 978-1-4296-1314-9 (hardcover)
    ISBN-10: 1-4296-1314-9 (hardcover)
    1. U-2 (Reconnaissance aircraft) — Juvenile literature. I. Title. II. Series.
UG1242.R4S9423 2008
623.74'67 — dc22   2007031328

Summary: Discusses the U-2 spy plane, its uses, engines, sensors, and future in
    the U.S. Air Force.

Editorial Credits
Matt Doeden, editor; Katy Kudela, photo researcher and revised edition editor;
    Kyle Grenz, revised edition designer

Photo Credits
AFFTC History Office, 1, 10, 24
Defense Visual Information Center (DVIC), cover, 28
Edwards AFB History Office, 6
Ted Carlson/Fotodynamics, 4, 9, 13, 16–17, 18, 20, 23, 27

1 2 3 4 5 6 13 12 11 10 09 08

Table of Contents

Chapter 1   The U-2 in Action 5
Chapter 2   Inside the U-2 11
Chapter 3   Sensors and Tactics 19
Chapter 4   Serving the Military...... 25

Features

U-2R Specifications........................ 15
Photo Diagram................................ 16
Glossary 30
Read More 31
Internet Sites................................ 31
Index 32

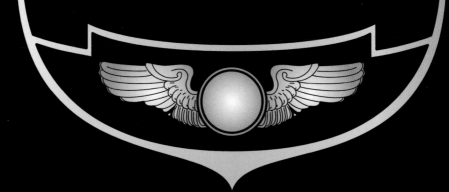

The U-2 in Action

Learn about

- The U-2's mission
- Military intelligence
- Early U-2 flights

It is a rainy night in an eastern European country. A group of soldiers is moving tanks and weapons toward the border of a neighboring country. The soldiers are preparing for a surprise invasion.

A black U-2 spy plane flies slowly in a wide circle 70 miles (113 kilometers) away. The plane is 12 miles (19 kilometers) above the ground. The soldiers below do not know that the U-2 is taking photographs of everything that they do.

The military designed the U-2 to gather intelligence.

On the other side of the world, three U.S. Air Force officers watch a computer screen. The officers are located at Beale Air Force Base in California. One of the U-2's photos appears on the screen. The officers realize that the enemy is planning an attack.

The Air Force officers send the photo to their leaders in Washington, D.C. Within hours, U.S. military forces in Europe are ready to defend against the attack.

Building the U-2

Military intelligence is information about an enemy's plans and actions. Intelligence is important to military leaders. They use it to prepare for and avoid battles. In the 1950s, U.S. military leaders wanted to build a spy plane to gather information about enemies. This action is called reconnaissance.

The U.S. military wanted a plane that could fly very high. It also wanted a plane that could fly long distances without stopping for fuel. Military leaders asked an aircraft builder called Lockheed Martin to build such a plane.

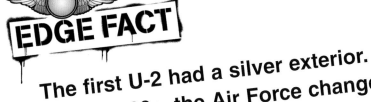

EDGE FACT

The first U-2 had a silver exterior. In the 1960s, the Air Force changed the outside of the plane to black.

Lockheed designed and built the U-2 in secret. The company tested the U-2 on a military base in Nevada and at Edwards Air Force Base in California.

Early History

The **Cold War** led to the development of the U-2. In 1956, the U-2 made its first reconnaissance flight over the Soviet Union. Today, the area that was the Soviet Union is split into Russia and several smaller countries. The U.S. military thought that there might be a war someday with the Soviet Union. U.S. military officials wanted to know everything they could about the Soviet military.

In 1960, the Soviet Union's military shot down a U-2. Soviet officials captured the plane's pilot, Francis Gary Powers. Powers later admitted that he had been spying on the Soviet Union. The Soviet government sentenced Powers to 10 years in prison. But the Soviet Union released him after just two years.

Cold War — a conflict between the United States and the country formerly known as the Soviet Union

The U-2R has built-in fuel tanks in its wings.

The U.S. military stopped flying U-2s over the Soviet Union after 1960. But it continued to use the plane elsewhere. In the 1960s, Lockheed built a bigger version of the U-2. It was called the U-2R.

The U-2R still is important for gathering intelligence. The U.S. Air Force has about 30 U-2Rs.

Inside the U-2

Learn about

- **U-2R specifications**
- **Body design**
- **Engine**

The U-2R does not look like any other U.S. military airplane. The U-2R's wingspan measures 105 feet (32 meters). Wingspan is the distance between the tips of the wings. Most military planes have a short wingspan. But the U-2R's wingspan is as long as the wingspans of some jet airliners.

The U-2R also is lightweight. It is lighter than some fighter planes. The U-2R weighs only about 14,900 pounds (6,759 kilograms) when empty.

Body Design

Lockheed designed the U-2R to be simple, dependable, and lightweight. The wings and body are made of a lightweight metal called aluminum. Tanks in the wings hold up to 9 tons (8 metric tons) of fuel.

The U-2R's body is designed to allow it to reach high altitudes. The U-2R's wings are long and straight. This gives the plane the highest possible lift.

The U-2R's long wings allow it to fly as high as 80,000 feet (24,400 meters). Flying at this altitude helps keep the U-2R safe from many enemy weapons. It also puts pilots in a good position to photograph the land below.

EDGE FACT

U-2Rs fly so high that heat from the sun is a problem for pilots. White sun shields over the cockpit help keep out the heat and glare.

The plane's fuselage is long and narrow. The narrow fuselage gives the plane a low amount of air resistance. This force of air slows down moving objects.

Designers built special landing gear for the U-2R. Most of the U-2R's weight is carried on a single two-wheeled landing leg. A small tailwheel helps to steer the plane on the ground.

Small landing gear makes the U-2R difficult to land.

Engine

The U-2R is powered by a single jet engine. This engine produces about 17,000 pounds (7,700 kilograms) of thrust. The engine's thrust pushes the airplane forward through the air.

A U-2R pilot pulls the plane into a steep climb after takeoff. The jet engine pushes the plane to its cruising altitude of 80,000 feet (24,400 meters). This climb may take less than 30 minutes. Pilots usually fly U-2Rs at about 460 miles (740 kilometers) per hour once they reach cruising altitude.

EDGE FACT

Pilots may spend many hours on a mission. They carry small containers of high-energy food with them. The containers look like toothpaste tubes.

Function:	High-altitude reconnaissance
Manufacturer:	Lockheed Martin
Deployed:	1967
Length:	63 feet (19.2 meters)
Wingspan:	105 feet (32 meters)
Height:	16 feet (4.9 meters)
Empty Weight:	14,900 pounds (6,759 kilograms)
Payload:	5,000 pounds (2,268 kilograms)
Engine:	One Pratt and Whitney J75-P-13B
Thrust:	17,000 pounds (7,700 kilograms)
Top Speed:	475 miles (765 kilometers) per hour
Ceiling:	80,000 feet (24,400 meters)
Range:	7,000 miles (11,300 kilometers)

A U-2R pilot must take care to keep the plane's engine running at high altitudes. The air at the U-2R's cruising altitude contains very little oxygen. Jet engines that do not receive enough oxygen stall. Stalled engines are difficult to restart at high altitudes. A U-2R pilot must keep the plane's speed high to force enough oxygen into the engine.

tail

fuel tank

tail wheel

wing

cockpit

nose

landing gear

Sensors and Tactics

Learn about

- **Spy equipment**
- **Payload**
- **Pressure suits**

U-2R pilots use a variety of sensors and scientific equipment to perform their missions. Sensors record information about what is happening on the ground below. U-2Rs may carry cameras, radar, radio antennas, and scientific equipment. Pilots use these sensors and equipment to gather information about an area.

U-2R pilots take photographs from high altitudes.

Sensors

The U-2R does not carry guns and missiles like most military planes. It carries sensors instead. U.S. military officials depend on information from U-2R sensors to learn about the enemy.

Cameras are the most important sensors for U-2R reconnaissance. In the 1950s and 1960s, U-2 pilots flew directly over targets to take photos. But today, U-2Rs have much more powerful cameras. Pilots can take photos of targets from as far as 100 miles (160 kilometers) away. Enemies rarely detect U-2Rs from this distance.

U-2Rs also carry many electronic sensors. These sensors include radar equipment and radio antennas. Radar uses radio waves to locate objects. Pilots use radar to create detailed maps of an area. They use the antennas to pick up enemy radio signals.

Most sensors are located along the plane's long nose or under the wings. Some sensors are located in an area behind the cockpit. U-2Rs can carry as much as 5,000 pounds (2,268 kilograms) of **payload**.

payload — the total weight of the equipment carried by an airplane

Adaptability

The sensors a U-2R carries depend on its mission. U-2Rs carry only the equipment they need.

Each mission requires different equipment. A night mission may require a radar device connected to powerful computers. The computers can make maps based on the information the radar device collects. A day mission may require a camera with a telescopic lens. The lens allows pilots to take detailed photographs from a great distance.

Other Equipment

The air at 80,000 feet (24,400 meters) does not contain enough oxygen for people to breathe. The U-2R's cockpit must be pressurized for pilots to survive. Machines pump air into the cockpit to keep air pressure high. But this is not enough. The cockpit cannot be pressurized if the U-2R's engine stops. The pilot might become unconscious before the engine could be restarted.

U-2R pilots wear pressure suits.

U-2R pilots must wear pressure suits to protect themselves from this danger. The suit covers the pilot's entire body. A pressure suit includes a helmet, a sealed visor, and heavy gloves. The suit provides air pressure to a pilot's body. A pilot wearing a pressure suit can survive even if a U-2R's engine stops. The pilot then has time to restart the engine.

Serving the Military

Learn about
- **Changes to the U-2R**
- **Additional U-2R uses**
- **Future plans**

The U.S. Air Force has been using U-2Rs for more than 40 years. Technology has changed a great deal since the U-2R was first used in the 1960s. The Air Force works to keep the U-2R up to date. New communication devices and sensors have kept the airplane useful through the years.

Updates

The Air Force is making several changes to keep the U-2R modern. The pilot controls inside the U-2R's cockpit are made up of dials and switches. Few modern airplanes include this kind of control system. The Air Force is changing the U-2R's controls. It is replacing the dials and switches with computer controls.

The Air Force also is updating the U-2R's sensors. Military leaders want immediate access to intelligence. Some U-2Rs now carry a satellite antenna. This device allows pilots to send information to a satellite orbiting earth. The satellite then can instantly send the information anywhere on earth.

EDGE FACT

The Air Force never gave the U-2R an official nickname. The "U" stands for utility.

Older U-2Rs have control systems with switches and dials.

New sensors also are making the U-2R more effective. Some new sensors are combinations of older sensors. For example, one new sensor combines radar information with infrared information. Infrared sensors detect heat. The combination of radar and infrared sensors can create pictures of objects inside thick forests.

The U-2R's Future

After many years of service, some military leaders believe it is time to retire the U-2R. Choosing a replacement plane is not easy. The U-2R has features not found in other aircraft. After careful research, the Air Force decided to slowly phase out the U-2R. Its replacement will be the Global Hawk, an **unmanned plane**.

The U-2R will not disappear completely from flight. Today, U-2Rs are used for more than just reconnaissance. Scientists sometimes use the planes for research. Scientists send equipment up with some U-2Rs to take measurements of Earth's atmosphere. U-2Rs have gathered information that has helped scientists learn about Earth's ozone layer. U-2R photos also have helped scientists study the effects of volcanic eruptions.

The U-2R will remain an important reconnaissance tool. Whatever the task, the U-2R will continue to soar high in the skies.

unmanned plane — a flying vehicle that carries no people and is controlled from the ground

GLOSSARY

Cold War (KOHLD WOR) — a conflict between the United States and the Soviet Union; the conflict lasted from about 1947 to 1990.

fuselage (FYOO-suh-lahzh) — the main body of an airplane

payload (PAY-lohd) — the total weight of the equipment carried by an airplane

pressurize (PRESH-uh-rize) — to seal off an airplane cockpit so that the air pressure is the same as pressure at the earth's surface

radar (RAY-dar) — equipment that uses radio waves to locate and guide objects

reconnaissance (ree-KAH-nuh-suhnss) — a mission to gather information about an enemy

unmanned plane (UHN-mand PLANE) — a flying vehicle that carries no people and is controlled from the ground

READ MORE

David, Jack. *U-2 Planes.* Torque Military Machines. Minneapolis: Bellwether Media, 2008.

Graham, Ian. *Warplanes.* The World's Greatest. Chicago: Raintree, 2006.

Hamilton, John. *The Air Force.* Defending the Nation. Edina, Minn.: Abdo, 2007.

INTERNET SITES

FactHound offers a safe, fun way to find Internet sites related to this book. All of the sites on FactHound have been researched by our staff.

Here's how:
1. Visit *www.facthound.com*
2. Choose your grade level.
3. Type in this book ID **1429613149** for age-appropriate sites. You may also browse subjects by clicking on letters, or by clicking on pictures and words.
4. Click on the **Fetch It** button.

FactHound will fetch the best sites for you!

INDEX

air resistance, 13

Beale Air Force Base, 6

cameras, 5, 6, 19, 21, 22
    telescopic lens, 22
cockpit, 12, 21, 22, 26
Cold War, 8
cruising altitude, 7, 12,
    14, 15

fuel tanks, 9
    capacity, 12
fuselage, 13

Global Hawk, 29

history, 7–9, 21, 25, 29

infrared sensors, 27

landing gear, 13
Lockheed Martin, 7, 8, 9,
    12, 15

manufacturer. *See*
    Lockheed Martin
materials
    aluminum, 12
missions, 5–6, 8, 14,
    19, 22

payload, 15, 21
Powers, Francis Gary, 8
pressure suits, 23

radar, 19, 21, 22, 27
radio antennas, 19, 21
reconnaissance, 7, 8, 21, 29

scientific research, 29
Soviet Union, 8, 9

U-2R features
    engine, 14, 15, 22, 23
    range, 7, 15
    speed, 14, 15
    weight, 11, 12, 13, 15
    wingspan, 11, 15